"*I am as a wonder. . .;
but thou art my strong refuge.*"

—PSALM 71:7.

I'm Glad to Be Me

by Barbara Shook Hazen
illustrated by Frances Hook

Library of Congress Cataloging in Publication Data

Hazen, Barbara Shook.
  I'm Glad to be me.

  A revision of the author's To Be me, published in 1975.
  SUMMARY: Children describe some of the things
that make them uniquely themselves and some of their feelings
about Jesus.
  [1. Individuality—Fiction.   2. Self-perception—
Fiction.   3. Christian life—Fiction]   I. Hook, Frances.
II. Title.
PZ7.H314975Im 1979   [E]   79-11726
ISBN 0-89565-074-6

Distributed by Standard Publishing, 8121 Hamilton Avenue,
Cincinnati, Ohio 45231.

THE
CHILD'S
WORLD ELGIN, ILLINOIS 60120

To be me
is to look in the mirror
and see me all pink
in my party dress.

Sometimes I wish
I had long hair like Ellen
or red shoes like Susie.
But most of the time
I'm glad to be me.

God made me different
from everyone else.

3

To be me
is to feel sad
because my kitten has a broken paw.

She doesn't like lollipops
so all I can do is hold her
and tell her I'm sorry she's hurt.

I love my kitten.

To be me
is to lie on my
back and watch
the clouds race
across the sky.

The sky is
so big, it makes
me feel small.

My teacher said
God made
everything.
Does that mean
God made the sky?

To be me
is to watch the rain
run down the window
in funny rivers.

I know ducks and frogs
and fish like the rain.
So do the trees and the flowers.
Is that why God sends the rain?

To be me
is to have a hurt
so bad it makes me cry.

Mommy puts on a bandage
and makes me feel better.
She always does.

Thank You, God, for Mommy.

To be me
is to make something
that's all mine
with clay or paper
or poster paint.

My picture doesn't look
like anybody else's,
the way I don't look
like anyone but me.

I like my picture.

To be me
is to feel shy
and too scared
to say, "Can
I play? Please
move over.
Make a space
for me. It's
no fun on the
outside."

Help me, God,
not to be afraid.

15

To be me
is to look at some of my things
and to be happy they are mine.

I put a ribbon, some bubble gum,
and a quarter in my purse.
I put a ring in there, too.

Sometimes I like things
just for me.
But I know I should share.
My mommy said so.
My teacher said so.
Jesus said so.

To be me
is to lie in the
grass and watch
a spider spin
a web of lace.

He sort of
scares me, but
I can't stop
watching him.

I wonder how
the spider learned
to make a web.
Did God tell him?

To be me
is to tug, tug, tug
and get mad at my boots
because they don't go on right.

When I'm grown
I'll never wear boots!

Mommy says I shouldn't get so mad.
She says Jesus will help me
to feel better
if I just ask Him.

To be me
is to feel the prickly, tickly touch
of Daddy's face, and to feel
his arms all warm around me.

I feel good when my Daddy
holds me tight and talks to me.
I know he loves me.

I know Jesus loves me, too.
I can't see Jesus,
but I know He's there.

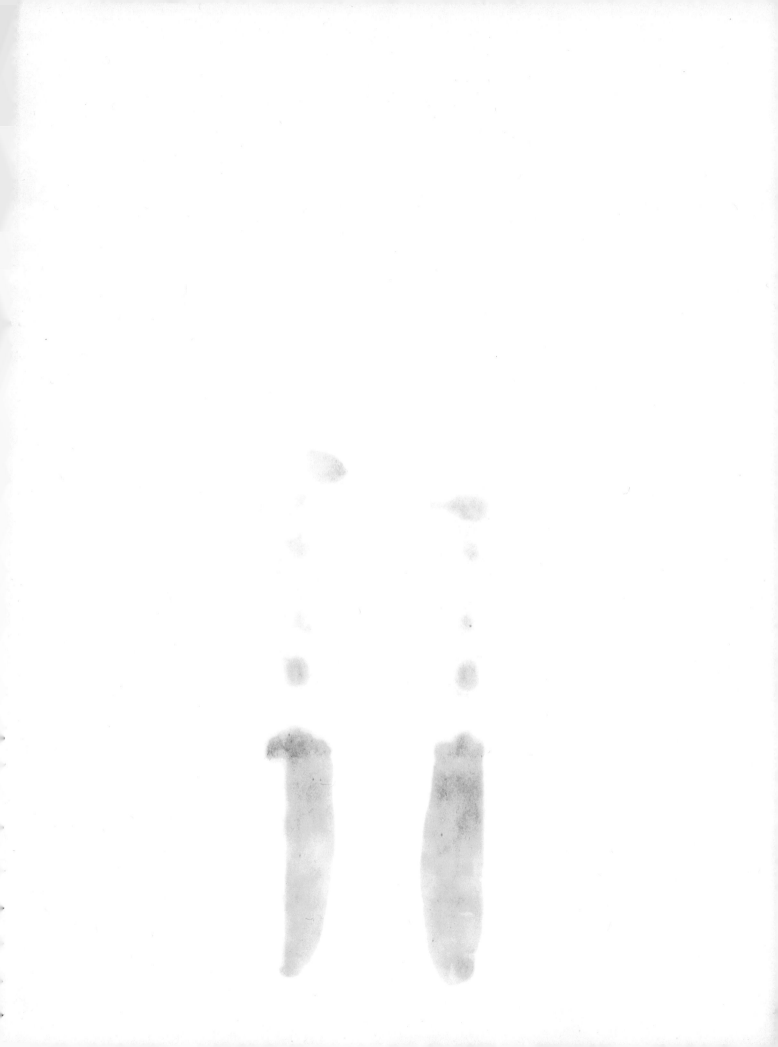

JUV HAZEN BARBARA SHOOK
Hazen, Barbara Shook
I'm Glad to be Me

Date Due

SEP 28 1980		DEC 1 1 1984	
OCT 1 4 1980	MAR 1 7 1981	APR 2 9 1986	
OCT 2 8 1980	SEP 1 5 1981	JAN 2 0 1987	
OCT 2 8 1980		FEB 1 0 1987	
	DEC 0 1 1981	NOV 1 0 1987	
NOV 1 1 1980	NOV 1 6 1982	MAY 2 0 1988	
NOV 2 5 1980	MAR 0 1 1983	SEP 2 0 1988	
JAN 2 0 1981		OCT 0 4 1988	
OCT 0 6 1981	APR 2 6 1983	10-20-90	
	NOV 1 1983	JAN 1 6 01	
MAR 1 6 1982			
	NOV 2 9 1983		

Concordia College Library
Bronxville, NY   10708